"Iowa State is such a special place. I'm thankful to Cyclone fans for their relentless enthusiasm and support, and for inspiring this story. And, to my beautiful wife, Joni, you are my inspiration every single day. I love you." —J.W.

First Edition
10 9 8 7 6 5 4 3 2 1

ISBN: print book 978-1-7369431-3-7
Library of Congress Control Number:2021938505

Publisher: Bob Snodgrass
Editor: Jennifer McDaniel
Publication Coordinator: Molly Gore
Sales and Marketing: Lenny Cohen
Dust Jacket, Book Design, and Illustrations: Rob Peters

The goal of Ascend Books is to publish quality works. With that goal in mind, we are proud to offer this book to our readers. Please notify the publisher of any erroneous credits or omissions, and corrections will be made to subsequent editions/future printings.

All stories, incidents, and dialogue are products of the imagination of the author and illustrator and are not to be construed as real. They are not intended to replicate actual historical events.

Officially licensed by Iowa State University

Printed in Canada

www.ascendbooks.com

CY'S™
Perfect
DAY

The Iowa State™ Way

John Walters
"Voice of the Iowa State™ Cyclones™"

Illustrated by
Rob Peters

ASCEND BOOKS
www.ascendbooks.com

It was a warm fall day in Cyclone Land.
The sunshine was bright and looking grand.
Cy jumped from his bed; he was so excited!
A new football season was about to begin,
     and Cy couldn't be more delighted.

Cy got ready. He rushed and he scurried.
Jack Trice Stadium would be full. There was no need to worry.
The Cyclones would win, he had no doubt.
A victory would be a great way for the season to start out.

Once Cy was at the stadium, he went
    looking for his friends.
Everyone was dressed in cardinal and
    gold, the game-day trend.
Soon he found Brad and Alicia in the tailgating lots.
"The Cyclones are going to win!" Brad exclaimed,
    while grilling up some brats.

Mel and Kathy were there, laughing
and sharing an Iowa State tale.
They too believed in an ISU win.
"Don't worry," they said. "The Cyclones will prevail!"

Friends Eric and Nicki also agreed.
Their entire family was on board.
"The Cyclones will chalk up a win," they said,
"but only if the crowd really roars."

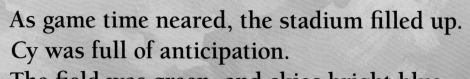

As game time neared, the stadium filled up.
Cy was full of anticipation.
The field was green, and skies bright blue—
all was right in Cyclone Nation!

The band played the fight song. The spirit squad cheered.
The loud, pumped-up crowd could be heard far and near.

And as the final seconds ticked away,
Cy found that his friends were right.
The Cyclones won! There was never a doubt.
They played with all their might.

Later that night, as Cy settled into bed, there was
just one thought that kept racing through his head.
"Today was simply the most perfect day.
A most perfect day in every way!"

When next week's game came,
it was more of the same.
Great times with his friends, high fives
and another big Cyclone victory in the end.

But when the next game came,
something was different.
It just wasn't the same.

Though his friends, the fans and the band were there, the team's chances of winning vanished into thin air.
And in the end, the Cyclones lost.
As Cy lay in bed that night, something kept bothering him.
He turned and he tossed.

The very next week those same
    thoughts raced through his head.
He started to worry. He began to fret.
"What if my friends don't come back,
    and decide to stay home instead?"
It was a thought he simply wanted to forget.

After all, we lost, and no one likes that.
"Will they be here on Saturday?
    Will they ever come back?"

When the next Saturday came, Cy jumped out of bed.
He anxiously waited for the moments ahead.
Cy was so nervous he couldn't eat.
Would his buddies and the fans be there to greet?

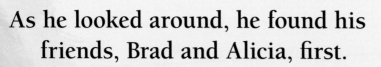

As he looked around, he found his
  friends, Brad and Alicia, first.
Cy was so happy! He was so joyful that he
  thought his heart might burst.
"I'm so glad you're back," he would say if he
  could, but Cy couldn't utter a word.
"Because we lost last week, no matter how hard we tried."
Would they understand his concern?

"But Cy," Alicia said. "Did you forget?"
"We're 'Clone to the bone. Forever and ever."
"Whether we win or we lose," Brad said.
   "That's how we'll always be.
   Once a Cyclone, ALWAYS a Cyclone.
   We're one, big family."

Cy couldn't believe it when he saw Mel and Kathy.
They were there, too. His heart swelled two
sizes bigger as they came into view.
"Of course, we're back, Cy, and our family, too.
We're loyal sons, FOREVER true!"

Kathy smiled and gave Cy a big hug,
which brightened his day.
"Don't worry," Mel said. "We'll win today!"

As Cy bounced to his next stop, he found Eric
    and Nicki with their family in tow.
They were ready for a Cyclone victory and
    wanted their team to steal the show.

"Why did you come back?" Cy thought to
    himself. "We lost the week before."
Nicki smiled, giving her friend a playful tap on
    the beak. "You really don't know what for?"
"Because my friend," Eric said. "Every day
    is a great day to be a Cyclone.
Some days are just a little bit better than the rest in the end."
"And today," Nicki said. "We'll make that last play.
Trust me, Cy, the Cyclones will win today."

Cy entered the stadium, bursting with pride.
His friends were back. They didn't run and hide.
Members of the Cyclone faithful,
    they fill the seats week after week.
Win or lose – to them, their team is
    always on a winning streak.

Once inside, he took a quick look around.
There wasn't an empty seat to be found!
It was just like it was before: the cheerleaders,
    the band, the bright blue skies.
Cy could feel tears coming to his eyes.

"This," Cy thought, "this is what being a Cyclone is all about.
My friends were right. There's no time to
    be sad. There's no time to pout."

And on that Saturday afternoon, the Cyclones played great.
They never gave up and rallied late.
Can you guess what happened? Can you guess how it ended?
Well, the Cyclones went out and won that day.
Jack Trice Stadium was rocking play after play.

And as Cy lay awake in bed that night, he couldn't
help but think how his friends were right.
Once a Cyclone, always a Cyclone. Win or lose.
We'll stay loyal sons, forever true.
Every day IS a great day to be a Cyclone, just like Eric said.
There was never a need to hang his head.

Cy did everything he could that
night to drift off to sleep.
He even tried counting fluffy, white sheep.
But try as he might, he just couldn't sleep.
He was too excited about the next day.
For it was the start of basketball
season just across the way.

It wouldn't be long before Hilton Magic
    would be alive and well.
He imagined all of the ISU fans he would
    see, and the buttery popcorn he'd smell.
All of his friends would be there too.
Those loyal sons, forever true.

Cy pulled up his blanket of
cardinal and gold, as he thought
to himself how Iowa State
games would never get old.

"We'll cheer on our Cyclones
every single day."
"We'll win a bunch, but we may lose
one or two along the way.
And you know what? That's OK.
"Because year after year, we'll always
return to those same seats, with those
same friends, convinced that this time,
the Cyclones will win once again."

And as Cy finally settled down to sleep that night, a final thought crossed his mind: "THIS really was a perfect day, a perfect way. The Iowa State way, day after day."